C.1 F F

Floethe, Louise

AUTHOR

Triangle X

TITLE

DATE DUE	BORROWER'S NAME	ROOM NUMBER
6 9	Rick Mexico	21
4 2	Jamie Aberes	17
5 1	Peggy Stark	24

C.1 F F

Floethe, Louise

Triangle X

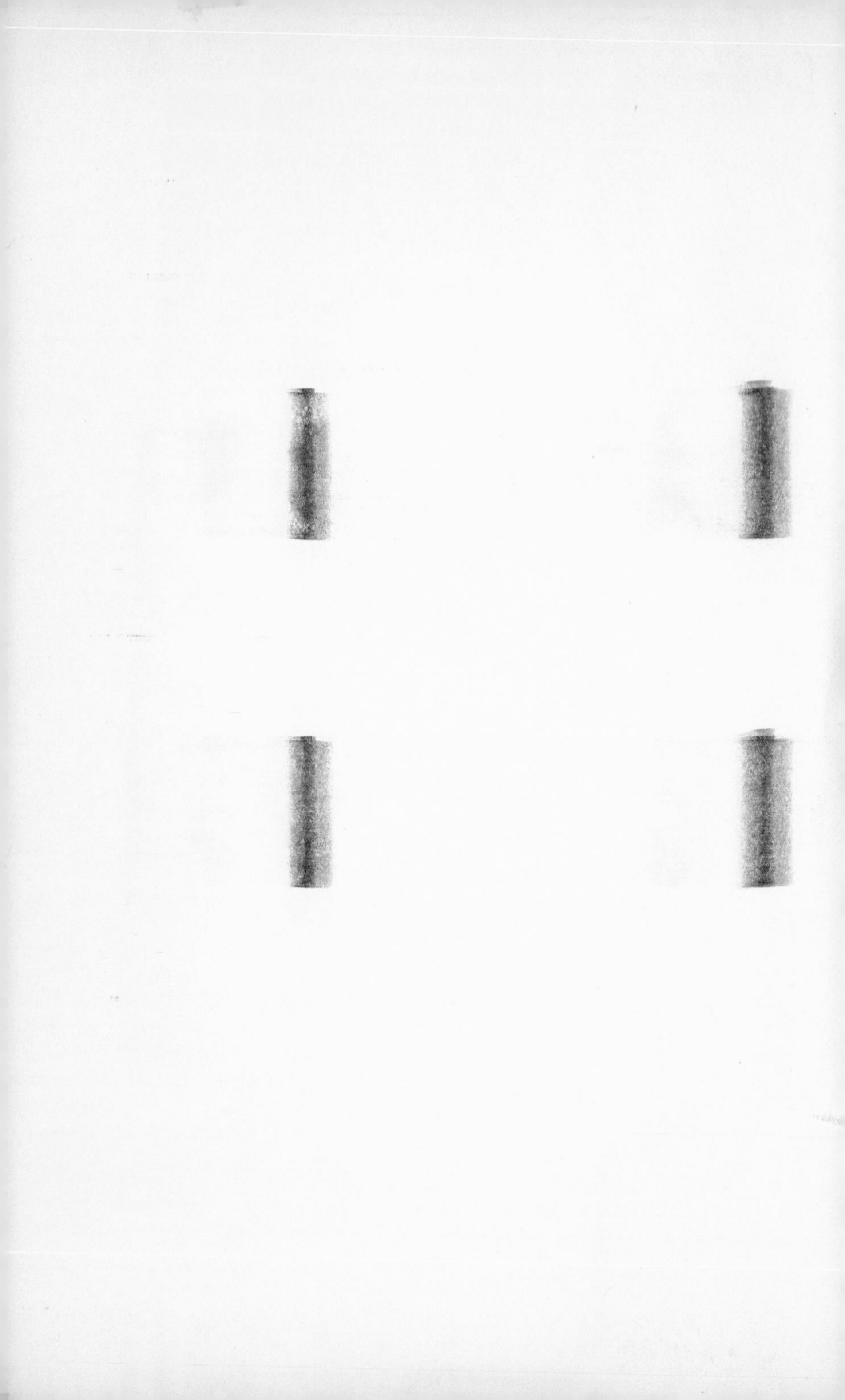

TRIANGLE X

TRIANGLE X

by Louise Lee Floethe

Pictures by Richard Floethe

HARPER & BROTHERS *Publishers* NEW YORK

TRIANGLE X

Printed in the United States of America

F-L

Library of Congress catalog card number: 60-5777

CHAPTER ONE

The plane flew high over the snow-capped mountains, then swooped down into the valley and landed.

Jeff unfastened his seat belt and stood up in the aisle.

"Got everything?" Jeff's father asked.

Jeff checked his hat, jacket, and book. He nodded.

"That sailor hat," said Jeff's mother, as they moved slowly toward the plane's exit, "is going to look a little funny out here in cowboy country, don't you think?"

Jeff shrugged a little uneasily.

The stewardess smiled. " 'Bye, sailor boy."

Jeff grabbed off his hat. The cool, thin mountain air blew through his hair. He took a deep breath. His heart raced excitedly. Was he really here in Wyoming? The snow on the tall, tall peaks glistened in the sun. Small planes dotted the airfield like colorful giant dragonflies. A horn honked welcome.

Jeff walked with his mother and father across the low-cut grass to where the cars were grouped near the small airport building.

"There!" cried Jeff. "The red station wagon. It says Triangle X Ranch on the door."

A smiling tall young man came toward them. "You must be the Mayberrys. I'm Nick Platter, chauffeur, errand-runner, fishing and pack trip guide and what have you for my folks at Triangle X Ranch."

Mr. Mayberry shook hands with Nick. "You must be a great help to your parents in running the ranch."

Nick shrugged. "Oh, my brother Ross and I

do our bit. Not that we really think of it as work. We like the ranch too much. School in the winter is the work part." Nick winked at Jeff as if to say, "You get my meaning, don't you, boy?" and then continued, "I'm at the University of Colorado and Ross will be a senior at high." And then, "If you'll give me your checks, I'll get your luggage to the car."

The red station wagon was almost the only car on the highway.

"It's twenty miles to the ranch," Nick said.

Jeff looked out the car window for a long while without speaking. Across the flats he saw twisted cottonwood trees growing along the shore of the coiling river. Bright flowers lined the road. Cattle grazed quietly between silvery sagebrush.

It was strange, thought Jeff, how he had just come down out of the sky from far, far away. He had been home in Florida the day before. Yesterday it had been palm trees and blue sea and sailboats. Today it was mountains and Nick Platter and—

"There," said Nick, pointing a finger, "there's Triangle X Ranch."

Jeff pressed his face against the window glass.

Nick swung the car off the highway and they bumped along a dirt road. He slowed to a creep over the cattle guard.

Triangle X Ranch! Yes, there it was. Somehow it looked just exactly the way Jeff knew it was going to look. There was the main house, a comfortable two-storied brown log building. And there were the small log guest cabins strung out down the slope, as if they were so many chicks the main house had hatched.

"Which is our cabin?" asked Jeff.

"Third from the end," said Nick. He drove the car right up to the porch.

"How cute," Mother said.

Jeff stumbled up the porch steps carrying his heavy duffel bag. He swung the screen door wide and stepped inside his bedroom. It was dark after the bright sunlight outside. He blinked. It was a fine room. The walls were of rough logs with nails driven in here and there to hang your clothes on. The bed was narrow with a colorful Indian spread on top. There was one bureau, one chair, and one rough wood table. There was a small chunk stove with the smokestack curving into the chimney. Piled on the floor were small-cut, yellowish-white logs and a big tin of sawdust soaked in kerosene for starting the fire.

On the other side of the wall Jeff heard his mother and father getting settled in their bedroom.

"Do I have to unpack everything now?" Jeff called.

"Might as well," his mother answered.

He couldn't wait to get out of his traveling clothes and into jeans and boots. They were stiff and shiny-new. He stomped across the porch self-consciously.

"How do I look?" Jeff asked.

"Swell," said his father, "like a real dude."

"Dude?" repeated Jeff. "Is that what I want to be?"

"I don't know if that's what you want to be, but that's what you are. We all are. Dudes. This is a dude ranch."

"What's a dude?" asked Jeff. "I mean, really." The word disturbed him.

"Dudes are people like us who spend a vacation on a ranch."

"Oh," said Jeff. He went out onto the cabin porch and stood staring at the great snow-capped mountains. A sudden scurrying noise startled him as a ground squirrel scampered across the lowest porch step and disappeared under the cabin. He reappeared shortly and in the friendliest fashion sat on his hind legs, twitched his pointed nose, and for all the world looked as if he were about to speak. "Does he know I'm a a dude?" Jeff wondered.

Suddenly from over the slope a line of horses came loping. In the lead a slim hard-muscled man wearing a faded blue shirt sat his saddle in the easy way that made Jeff know right away that he belonged. The rest of the riders were dudes of course. Jeff watched until the last of them disappeared behind the ranch house to the corral.

Jeff walked up the slope to the corral. His new boots felt hard and uncomfortable. But he did not think of his boots. He thought of the way the man and his horse looked as if they'd both been out in the weather a lot. As if they knew just where they were going and how to get there. They were strong like the jagged rock of the mountains. And they were wild somehow, like the wind blowing cold from the snowy peaks.

The dudes were strolling from the corral.

"Hi." They smiled at Jeff.

Jeff approached the high wooden fence around the corral and peered between the boards. The man with the faded blue shirt moved easily among the corraled horses, loosening the cinches on the horses which were to remain saddled for the afternoon ride. "Hey, Val, that lady going to ride Chink this afternoon?"

"Nope. Said she was going fishing."

In a twinkling the saddle was unhitched and slid from the back of the small brown and white pinto. Then the bridle was slipped from his head. The little horse gave a grateful shake. The man carried the bridle and saddle into the tack room, deposited the saddle on a rack, and tied the bridle to the saddle horn. As he sauntered back into the dusty brown corral he stopped to light a cigarette. The flame from his match lit up his deeply sun-tanned skin, and Jeff saw that his eyes were a pale gray-blue under the wide brim of his felt hat.

A boy of about sixteen, with heavy horn-rimmed glasses and the look about him of a young scientist, strolled easily over to Jeff. "I'm Ross Platter," he said, shaking hands. "You're new, aren't you?"

Jeff scuffed at the dirt with his shiny new boots.

"Yes," he said, "I'm Jeff Mayberry." Then, "Who is that man?" he asked.

Ross peered quickly between the boards of the fence. "The one in the blue shirt? That's Hugh. He's our head wrangler."

"Wrangler?" said Jeff in alarm. "I thought he was a cowboy."

"Nope. Wrangler. Wranglers are the ones who take care of the horses. Cowboys take care of the cattle. The one in the plaid shirt, he's Val. And the other wrangler is Luke. They're real good guys. Luke likes to tease a bit. He's part Indian."

Jeff listened carefully.

"You don't have a horse yet, do you?" asked Ross.

Jeff shook his head.

"Well, go on in and ask Hugh. He'll fix you up with a good one." Ross pushed open the corral gate.

Jeff walked slowly into the corral.

Ross closed the gate after him. "See ya," he called cheerily.

The wranglers glanced at Jeff briefly and went on with their work.

Jeff stood in the dusty passage between tack

room and enclosed area for the horses. The air was heavy with the smell of horses and dust and sweat-stained leather. He had never been close to so many horses all at once. There must have been forty or fifty in the enclosure. All colors. Some tall. Some short. All carrying the brand of Triangle X Ranch on their hindquarters.

A horse leaned over and nipped its neighbor. Hoofs flew. The horses crowded in on one another.

"Steady, there!" Hugh's voice called above the confusion. The flat of his hand smacked the offender.

The horses quieted.

How sure Hugh was, Jeff thought. Everything about his tall, lean body was sure. Even the way his faded blue shirt hung loosely from his shoulders and swung with him as he moved had about it a kind of dash and freedom that Jeff found fascinating.

Hugh carried the last saddle to the tack room. "Hi," he said, and smiled at Jeff.

Luke scuffed up behind Hugh, his black Indian eyes twinkling at Jeff. "Got us a new dude, eh?"

Jeff nodded. "I want a horse," he said boldly.

And then suddenly wished he had held his tongue.

"A horse?" said Hugh, as if the word were new to him. "You're wanting a horse?"

Jeff nodded again.

Hugh's eyes traveled slowly from the top of Jeff's head down to the tips of his boots covered now with a thin film of red-brown Wyoming dust. "Can you ride?" he asked slowly, not unkindly.

"Some," Jeff answered. "I rode at camp last summer. But only on an English saddle."

"One of them flat skinny little things?" Luke asked.

"Yes."

"Beats me how a man can ride 'em. It's a shame to waste good leather on one of them postage stamps."

"I saw a man once taking high jumps in an English saddle," remarked Hugh. "Let me tell you that man could ride." Then, smiling slowly at Jeff, "I got a proposition to make to you, boy. How about this afternoon my saddling you up a real quiet mare I got here. Then, when I can see how well you ride, I'll assign you a horse for your stay. That O.K.?"

This wasn't exactly the way Jeff had expected it

to be. A nice quiet horse always meant the oldest and the slowest in the string. Still, he looked back up into Hugh's level gray-blue eyes watching and judging him, and said cheerfully, "O.K."

"Good," said Hugh.

Just then the pounding of a gong rang out from the main house.

"Lunch," said Luke. "Better hurry before the food's all gone."

"Hey," called Hugh.

Jeff looked back.

"What'd you say your name was?"

"Jeff."

"Mine's Hugh." He held out his work-roughened hand.

Jeff grasped the hand proudly. "Pleased to meet you," he said politely. Then he ran to the ranch house for lunch.

CHAPTER TWO

Hugh kept Jeff riding the "real quiet mare" for several days. Each morning, as Jeff swung into the saddle and smoothed the tangled mane over the tired, stubborn, old neck, he thought that surely today Hugh would assign him the horse he had promised for his stay. Several times he had almost asked, "Say, when do I get my regular horse, anyway?" But there was something about the way Hugh looked at him from time to time as they rode out that always made him hold his tongue.

Not that Hugh was stern or frightening in any way. It was just that his clear gray-blue eyes seemed to judge a fellow. Jeff wanted Hugh to like him more than anyone he'd ever met.

Jeff worked as hard as he could at riding the mare well. He sat up very straight in the saddle. He kept his knees tight and his heels down as much as he could. The mare, for all that she was old and quiet, was not easy to ride. In the first place she was barn sour. She did not like leaving the peace of the corral for a long trek across country. In her stubborn old way she tried every trick she knew to turn around and head back. Jeff had to pound his heels into her to keep her moving. Then, once they were on their way, she poked along as slow as she could. She hated to trot. But she did it when all the other horses began. But cantering, no! She made it very plain that she was too old for that kind of nonsense. Let the younger, sillier horses thunder across the flats kicking up swirls of red dust. This was not for her. She sneezed loudly, shook her head, and went no faster than a jog.

Jeff would get so angry he could almost have

cried. The idea of everyone else cantering and he doomed to jog-trot along was really very trying. No matter how he pounded his heels or angrily slapped the reins on her neck or yelled at the top of his lungs, the old beast went along at her own sweet rate. The worst of it all was that sometimes, while kicking so hard, Jeff would lose his balance and have to grab the pommel of the saddle to keep from falling off. Why was it that at times like that Hugh always seemed to be watching?

But even if the old horse annoyed him, Jeff enjoyed the rides across country. There were usually about ten dudes with one wrangler to watch over them. They always rode in single file because of the narrow trails. They never seemed to go on the same trail twice. They could ride for miles and never see another human soul.

And the land they traveled over was very different. There were the flats down by the winding river. They were dusty when it had not rained for several days, but they were made for fast travel. Sometime, when he got his real horse, Jeff knew that he too would gallop across the flats, fast and free with the wind whipping his hair.

There were the woods where they could do little

but walk. Branches hung low and sometimes snapped across the face. There were only two kinds of trees. Pine and white-barked aspen with shimmery silver leaves trembling at the faintest wind. The ground was brilliant with flowers. Jeff liked to breathe deeply of the woodsy air, rich with the odor of wild growing things.

There were the giant buttes—round, treeless hills, looking like the dome of a bald man's head. Too steep to climb straight up. They zigzagged their way up the buttes. At the top the great country opened up beneath them. They could see the river snaking its way through the flats, the twisted cottonwood trees growing along its banks, and a huge black raven circling, circling, looking for food. Then down again the steep, steep way. Even sitting in the saddle, the backs of Jeff's legs and his knees ached with the strain. He was happy when Hugh called for a rest and they climbed off their horses and threw themselves on the dry, baked ground.

The horses immediately began to nibble at the short, dry grass.

"They won't run off home?" asked a new dude.

"Nope," said Hugh. "They'll stand by." He gave Jeff a wink, then, stooping, he plucked off a twig of sagebrush and threw it into Jeff's lap.

Jeff liked the strong spicy smell. He brought the twig close to his nose.

"The horses don't eat that stuff, do they?" asked the new dude.

"Nope. Nothin' does, except the prairie chicken."

"Too bad, when there's so much of it, to have it all useless."

Hugh pushed his big hat to the back of his head. "Oh, I dunno. I'd kinda miss it if it weren't there."

A lady dude laughed and said, "Isn't there a cowboy song called 'Is There Sagebrush in Heaven'?"

"I don't rightly know," Hugh answered, "but I guess that's about the way we all feel about it."

Jeff looked down the slope to where miles of sagebrush sprawled across the range. It was like a silver sea rippling softly in the breeze. A few days ago he'd never in his life seen or even heard of sagebrush. Now, he, too, felt he'd miss it if it weren't there.

Little by little Jeff spent more and more time in the corral with Hugh and the other wranglers.

There never seemed an end to the things to do. Before the morning ride there were about forty horses to saddle and bridle. Jeff liked to get up earlier than his parents and sneak out of the cabin into the still dewy, nippy morning and run to the ranch house to have breakfast with the wranglers. Later he could go with them to the corral and help with the saddling.

Of course the wranglers had been working since long before breakfast. They had to get up about five, saddle the horses they kept overnight in the barn, and ride out on the range to wrangle up the *remuda*. All night long the horses had been feeding. Only the wranglers' horses which were kept in the barn were fed oats. All the rest searched out their own food on the wide range.

"And good food it must be," Jeff's father had pointed out, "because I've never seen healthier horses."

The cold, early morning ride made the wranglers very hungry. Jeff could never get over the marvel of seeing them down two or three eggs each, lots of brown, crisp bacon, platters of toast, and heaps of pancackes dripping with syrup. And all of this washed down with what seemed like gallons of the blackest coffee Jeff had ever seen.

"Eat, boy," they would urge him, and drop a second egg on his plate.

Jeff often made a fuss about eating eggs at home. But under Hugh's level gaze he manfully swallowed what they put on his plate.

Hattie, the cook, who ruled her kitchen and all the hired help on the ranch with a hand of iron, stuck her head around the stove, where she continued to turn pancakes, and warned, "Jeff, drink your juice. You have to have vitamins." She did not seem to care if the wranglers had vitamins or not.

Jeff drank his juice. Then he went with the wranglers, out of the warm, good-smelling kitchen, to the corral.

Then came one particular morning. It started like all the others. The corral looked the same as usual with horses crowding one upon the other. Luke and Val had lost no time getting to the tack room and lugging out saddles and bridles. They slipped the bit between the horse's teeth; brought the bridle up over the head and ears; slapped the saddle blanket on the horse's back; fitted the saddle on top; brought the cinch loosely around under the belly; and turned their attention to the next horse. Later, just before the dudes mounted, they would tighten the cinches and re-check the equipment.

Jeff hurried to the tack room. Just as he was about to step over the pine-log sill, his eye was caught by Nick and Ross Platter at the far end of the corral fussing over a beautiful sorrel mare and her wobbly newborn colt. Jeff forgot about helping the wranglers saddle. He ran around the fence to the brothers.

"Where does she come from?" he asked the Platters.

Ross ran his hands down the mare's legs. His dark eyes were serious behind his large black owl-like glasses. "They brought Bee in from the range this morning."

"Oh, are there more horses out on the range?" asked Jeff. He had thought that the wranglers brought in all the *remuda* each morning.

"A few," answered Ross. "The mares that are breeding and any horses we're giving a rest." He jerked his finger behind him. "That fellow there's just had a vacation."

Jeff looked around, and there was a horse he had not seen before. He was a stocky, well-built bay with an odd white marking running straight

down the length of the center of his back. Jeff liked the look of him at once.

"What's his name?" he asked.

"Skunk," said Ross, rising from his examination of the mare's legs.

The mare turned anxiously and gave a reassuring nip to her little colt's flanks.

"Skunk!" repeated Jeff.

"Yeah, he's called that because of the white marking down his back," Ross answered, then seriously to his brother, "The old girl's legs seem as good as ever. I wonder if we'll dare use her for the Dude Rodeo?"

"What Dude Rodeo?" questioned Jeff.

Nick smiled. He was used to questions. It was part of running a dude ranch to answer them. "Next month over at Camp Robbins there'll be a contest. The ranches for miles around compete. Races for kids under twelve. For over twelve. Pack races. Milk races. All kinds of events."

"Oh," said Jeff, "are you and Ross going to be in it?"

"Nope. We don't qualify. Only dudes can be in it. Each ranch picks the best dudes available for each event."

"Gee," said Jeff, not daring to hope that he might be in it.

"Nick and I train the dudes," Ross said.

"And boy, do we train them!" Nick added. And then they both laughed.

The little colt nuzzled at his mother for milk.

"I sure hope we can use Bee," Ross said, shaking his wise young head. "She's the fastest horse we have on the ranch."

"Hey," called Hugh, who was standing at the door to the tack room, "I got a different saddle and bridle for you today, Jeff. Come here and I'll show you."

Jeff ducked under the corral enclosure and ran to Hugh. This was certainly a morning for things happening! He felt a little breathless.

"Where?"

"Number 36," Hugh said, pointing down the line of racks. "You'll find this saddle's a bit smaller than your other one."

"Why?"

Hugh stopped to light a cigarette. A slight smile curled the corners of his mouth. "Well," he drawled, "I reckon because Skunk's a smaller horse than the mare. Fit him better, that's all."

"Skunk!" Jeff couldn't help shouting his joy.

"Yep," said Hugh, "he's your horse now."

"Skunk," repeated Jeff happily.

Proudly he lifted the saddle from the rack and lugged it to the corral. Because of the odd white marking down the center his back, he spotted Skunk at once among the mass of horses. As he made his way through the corral he passed the old mare. He gave her hindquarters an affectionate shove with his shoulder. But his eyes were on Skunk. There was no room in his mind now for anything but Skunk.

CHAPTER THREE

"Hey there, boy, you'll rub the hide off that horse cleanin' him so much," Luke teased.

Jeff paused as he currycombed. He pushed his new big felt hat to the back of his head the way Hugh did, and grinned at Luke. "I want him to look nice," he said.

"You betcha," Luke nodded. He yawned widely. "I'm gonna hit the sack. Think those horses can live without me till we're on the trail for the picnic this evening?"

"You betcha," Jeff answered right back.

Luke swung open the gate to the corral. "Wrangling dudes," he muttered, shaking his head. "Fine occupation for a grown man!"

The gate creaked shut. Jeff laughed. Luke loved to complain about working on a dude ranch. This was his first summer at it. He'd always been on real working cattle ranches before, and in the winter, of course, he'd be going back to one. But, in spite of his complaints, Jeff knew that Luke really liked cracking jokes with the dudes. As Hugh said, "People are almost as interesting as horses. And you meet all kinds on a dude ranch."

Skunk twitched his skin against a bothersome fly. Jeff started to comb out his tangled mane. He was a wonderful horse and Jeff loved him dearly. He deserved to have the snarls combed from his mane and tail and the heavy brown dust brushed out of his coat. Skunk was a special horse and he deserved special treatment.

Of course there wasn't time to give each horse in the *remuda* this kind of care. Only three wranglers minding fifty-odd horses. It was work enough just saddling and bridling them all. The rain and the dew or a splash in a deep gully were all the cleaning these horses got. They all had a rough, weather-beaten look to them. They reminded Jeff, somehow, of his old teddy bear, after he'd forgotten him and left him out all night in the rain, and his mother had hung him on the clothesline to dry.

Skunk hung his head sleepily. It was hot in the afternoon sun. The horses in the corral bunched together and slept on their feet. Only now and again they whisked their tails or twitched their skin under the heavy saddles. Jeff yanked and yanked at the snarls in Skunk's mane.

"There, that's better now, isn't it?"

But Skunk did not seem to care. His lids closed heavily over his soft brown eyes.

It had already turned cool by the time they set out for the picnic. Jeff wore a sweater, and his heavy jacket was tied behind the saddle with leather straps. He'd be glad of that later. Once the sun dipped behind the great mountains it got really cold.

It was quite a sight to see them all start out from the ranch. Fifty horses in single file. Everyone came to the picnics. All the dudes. And the Platter family. And all the help on the ranch. The wranglers had driven two trucks down earlier to the picnic site with all the provisions needed. They had started three fires for the cooking and set the enormous pots of water for coffee on to boil. Then they had bounced the trucks back over the rutted roads leading through the flats, making it to the ranch just in time to mount everyone for the ride.

Jeff loved the way Skunk moved. He never had to kick and kick him the way he had the old mare. Just a gentle signal with Jeff's heels and a tightening of the reins was enough for Skunk to know what was expected of him. He had a nice, fast walk. He held his head high and his sensitive nostrils quivered. He always knew everything that was going on around him. Many times Skunk saw things long before Jeff did.

Hugh let Jeff ride right behind him in the lead of the *remuda.*

"You can be my gate-opener," Hugh had said.

And Jeff was very proud of this honor.

The first gate came about a half-mile from the ranch, just before they reached the highway.

Jeff slipped from his saddle, took Skunk's reins over his arm while he pushed the wire loop up the post, and swung the gate wide open. He and Skunk stood by the gate as the entire *remuda* passed through. Then once more he fastened the wire loop, remounted Skunk, and galloped to the head of the line just behind Hugh.

On the other side of the highway they passed through a second gate, and later, down where the willows grew thickly in boggy land, they came to another.

Luke grinned down at Jeff standing beside Skunk, as the horses filed past. "Hi there, crumb-pusher," he said.

Later, when he'd galloped back beside Hugh at the head of the line, Jeff asked him, "What's a crumb-pusher?"

Hugh looked a little surprised. "Someone call you that?" he asked.

"Luke."

Hugh nodded. Then he leaned over and straightened the rein on Skunk's neck. "A crumb-pusher is someone who helps in small ways. Runs errands, does the little pesky jobs." Hugh patted Skunk's neck affectionately. "You gotta be a crumb-pusher before you get to be a regular hand, Jeff. Don't forget that." Hugh gave him a smile before he pulled ahead on the trail.

Skunk broke into a fine lope behind Hugh's horse. The sound of many galloping hoofs

thudded behind. The dust swirled in a brown cloud. Forward, forward they pressed, sure of foot, fast and free. Nothing in the world was nicer than this, Jeff thought. A startled antelope leaped from a thicket of willow and raced wildly ahead of them to the safety of distance.

Hugh slowed the *remuda* to a walk before coming to the picnic site. It was a fine spot at the edge of the winding river beneath a group of twisted cottonwood trees. The wranglers had roped off a corral for the horses. The fires welcomed with the sweet smell of burning pine. Hattie and some of her kitchen help had already arrived by truck and were setting up great bowls of food on two weather-beaten wooden tables. As soon as the wranglers had the horses safely corraled they set about cooking.

Each fire was in a hollowed-out scoop of earth so that no embers could blow. Over the first fire the water for the coffee was coming to a boil. Over the second fire there was a grate and on this went a huge frying pan filled with cooked potatoes. It was Val's job to flip the potatoes until they turned a crisp brown. On the third fire was a griddle for the cube steaks. Hugh presided over these, getting them off the griddle while they were still rare and tasty. Luke took care of the coffee. He dumped the grounds right into the giant pot of boiling water. Then he placed a twig over the top of the pot to cut the bubbles as they rose to the surface. This kept the coffee from boiling over.

Jeff heaped his paper plate with some of all the good food. He sat down on a log next to Nick and Ross.

One of the dudes spoke to the Platter boys. "Hear you're taking a party out on a pack trip in the morning."

"Just for overnight," Ross answered. "Up to Silver Lake. We'll get in a bit of fishing and see a lot of wild life."

"Gets pretty cold at night though, doesn't it?"

Ross shrugged. "Yeah. But we'll have our sleeping bags."

"Ever see any bears?"

"Sure. Plenty."

Jeff stared at the Platter boys. How wonderful, he thought, to be able to talk about fishing and sleeping bags and bears just as if they were all part of everyday life. How he wished that he could go with them on this pack trip! But of course they wouldn't want any young boys along. It was useless even to ask.

The dude moved along. Ross turned to Jeff and, peering at him through his heavy black-rimmed glasses, asked, "How do you like that horse of yours?"

Jeff quickly swallowed a huge piece of steak. "Skunk? Oh, he's swell!"

Ross nodded. "Yeah. He used to be my horse until I got the palomino colt."

"Oh." Jeff felt very proud that he had been trusted with a horse that had once belonged to Ross. He thought of this as he finished his meal.

All at once everyone was putting on extra jackets. The sun had slipped behind the great mountains, and it was cold. The wranglers lighted the big campfire and everyone gathered around. A young man with a guitar stood before the fire and sang to them. His songs were sad and sweet and told mostly of the loneliness of the cowboy's life. Behind the singer and the fire and the wide, winding river, rose the great mountains. They looked as if some giant hand had cut them from deep purple paper and stuck them up against the dark blue sky.

A little shiver ran through Jeff. It was not a shiver because of cold. It was a shiver because suddenly he had thought how beautiful it all was. And how strange and marvelous that he, Jeff Mayberry, was really and truly here!

It was very dark when they mounted for the ride home. But even so the wranglers knew each horse and who was riding it. Before the riders mounted, the wranglers tightened the cinches.

"Want to open and shut gates on the way home?" Hugh asked Jeff.

"Sure!"

"O.K. You can carry my lantern then."

It was the only light in the great darkness. There was no moon, and the stars glimmered palely through strips of dark clouds. The darkness and the silence surrounded them. No one spoke. There was only the friendly creak of leather and the soft thud of hoofs.

Skunk walked briskly behind Hugh's horse. They took a short way home, cutting across a shallow gully. How completely sure-footed these horses were! Down the steep bank, over the slippery rocks, up again on the far side. They never hesitated. The *remuda* came on behind them single file. They could see the red beam of the lantern Jeff carried to the very end. It was a cheerful sign to follow.

Jeff had only two gates to open and close on the way back.

"Hi! Nice work." Jeff recognized Nick Platter's voice as he rode through the gate.

"Hi," he called back into the darkness.

When the last of the *remuda* had passed through, Jeff remounted and trotted forward to the lead just behind Hugh. He felt pleased with the way Nick had greeted him.

The lights of the ranch welcomed them. Everyone was grateful to dismount in the corral and go to the comfort and warmth of the little cabins. The wranglers and the Platter boys still had all the unsaddling to do.

"Please, may I stay and help?" Jeff begged his mother.

"You've had such a long day," she answered doubtfully.

"Oh, let him," said his father. "But don't be too long."

Happily Jeff lugged saddles to the tack room. Floodlights made the corral almost as bright as day. But the daytime joking was absent. Everyone was cold and tired and anxious to call it a day.

Nick rested his hand on Jeff's shoulder as they came out of the tack room together. "You're a real worker, Jeff," he said. There was a kind of wonder in his voice, as if he hadn't expected to find that in a dude. "Like to have you on our pack trip tomorrow, if you'd care to come," he continued.

Care to come! Jeff almost exploded, "Would you really take me?"

"Sure thing." Then, calling across the corral to his brother, "Hey, Ross, I've asked Jeff here to go with us on the pack trip tomorrow."

Ross paused as he unsaddled, to shove his heavy glasses up his nose. "Great," he called back. "We'll be leaving at seven."

CHAPTER FOUR

They could not travel fast because of the pack horses. They plodded along single file, silent in the early morning brightness. Never had the mountains looked so clear, so close. Not a single cloud softened the blueness of the sky. Each dew-drop glistened. Indian paintbrush flamed across the slopes.

Skunk held his head high and blew his nostrils wide. Jeff patted his neck. Off in the distance

Jeff saw a cabin. It looked as lonely and forgotten as a bleached bone.

"What's that?" Jeff asked Nick, who rode just ahead of him.

"Outlaws' cabin," Nick answered.

"Oh! Are they still there?"

"Nope. The last of them got shot up about fifty, sixty years ago. You see this valley used to be a hiding-out place for rustlers. Being surrounded by mountains the way it is, it was a hard place to get to. But the sheriff and his deputies cleaned out the last of the rustlers in a battle right inside that cabin."

A quiver of excitement ran through Jeff. "Can you still see the blood?"

"Well—not exactly. Why don't you ride up there and have a look? Lope back and meet us due west. You'll always know which way west is by the mountains."

That was all Jeff needed. Pulling his wide hat more squarely down on his head, he set heels to a willing Skunk, and cantered off across the range.

As he drew near the outlaws' cabin he was a shade disappointed. It was only an ordinary log building with clay stuffed between the cracks. It was weathered as gray as sagebrush. He did not know why, but somehow he had expected an outlaws' cabin to look different.

Jeff slipped from the saddle and dropped the reins. Skunk started to graze immediately. Jeff walked toward the cabin. Quite suddenly he was gripped by an odd feeling. What was it? The silence? The aloneness? He paused and stood still. In the distance the great mountains towered. All around the cabin lay a great flat sea of land. A few stubby, windswept clumps of willows trembled in the morning breeze. As far as Jeff's eyes could see there was nothing, nothing but the cabin itself, to show that man had ever been there.

Jeff began to hum to give himself courage. It was silly of course. There was nothing here. Just an old cabin. And yet—men had been killed here in a bloody shooting battle. Of course there were no such things as ghosts—but—but still—?

He stopped short as he heard a rustling sound. His heart began to beat. He looked back at Skunk grazing unconcernedly. Then he saw what it was. Over the cabin's empty yawning doorsill two ground squirrels scampered. Jeff felt better immediately. He decided to go in and look the cabin over.

There were two rooms with a kind of covered courtyard between them. The rooms were just the same in size. Each had a fireplace and three small windows close under the roof. The floors were of sod. In one room stood the remains of crude bunks and a table. That was all. It smelled damp and cold and musty.

It was nothing special. Just an old cabin. Then he saw the bullet holes spattered across one wall. A cold shiver went down his spine.

He stuck his finger into one of the bullet holes. Men had stood here once with shots ringing out all around them. They had been frightened and desperate. Surely they had fought back, shooting out from the small, high windows, maybe wounding or killing one of the sheriff's deputies.

Suddenly it all seemed very close and very real. The silence which weighed so heavily around the deserted cabin now must have been the same in the days when the rustlers had hidden out here. Every day they must have scanned the horizon anxiously for signs of the law coming in pursuit. And for a long time there had been nothing but the mountains and the endless range. They had had to live with the snow and the wind howling down the valley and the sudden violent rains. They had had to live with the loneliness.

And then all at once the sheriff and his deputies had come. The great silence and the loneliness was shattered by a burst of gunfire. In the end the men lay dead.

Jeff was happy to move out of the damp, dark room into the fresh sunlight. He mounted Skunk and loped back to the party.

After a while they left the sage slopes and entered the woods. They climbed steadily, following long, winding, dim trails. It was a wonder to Jeff how Nick and Ross always knew exactly where they were going. As they rode Ross pointed out the wild flowers. They had odd names like fleabane and fern-leaf lousewart and monkshood. Ross knew them all. His sharp eyes, behind the heavy lenses, searched constantly for rare flowers for his collection. He also knew the habits of the wild animals. He showed them moose tracks and the sharp clawings of bear on the spruce bark. He spoke angrily of the damage done by porcupines. They liked to eat the bark off the lower part of the pine, leaving a wound from which the sap flowed until death overtook the tree. He spoke grimly of the porcupine he had killed and what he would like to do to the whole race of destructive creatures.

Now and again Nick called a rest and they dismounted gratefully and stretched their aching legs and knees. The horses immediately nibbled the lush grass which grew knee-deep. They did not eat the flowers.

At noon the party was hungry for the picnic lunch Hattie had packed for them. They had sandwiches, a hard-boiled egg, cookies, and an orange. Jeff was so hungry he could have eaten more. After lunch they remounted and continued the steady climb up the mountain.

At length they came out of the heavy timber and came down upon Silver Lake. Why it was called Silver Lake, Jeff could not imagine, because the water was a bright blue-green in color. It was a beautiful lake, about half a mile across, with pebbly shores. Upon the opposite side were beaver mounds. Ross showed them where big trout were swimming around. Everyone in the party immediately became eager to get to his fishing rod.

First, however, they set up camp. Ross and Nick pitched the small tents and set up the cooking gear. Jeff was sent to collect firewood. The horses were hobbled and then turned loose to graze around the camp.

Soon everything was under control, and they all took off eagerly to try their fishing luck. Each one picked what he considered a favorable spot and began at once to cast into the icy clear water. Jeff watched Ross where he stood on a large rock. His arm swung back for a splendid cast. Almost instantly the water boiled and he hooked a good-sized trout. Jeff shouted with excitement and watched with admiration as Ross played the fish skillfully and at last beached him. He was a cut-throat trout, silvery-sided and marked with a red slash along his gill. Jeff could not help but wish that this was his fish.

Jeff continued along the lake shore until he was alone. He knew that he was awkward at casting and he did not want the others to see him. He took off his shoes and socks and rolling up his jeans waded into the freezing water. At first he thought his feet would turn into blocks of ice, but after a short time he grew used to it. He put all his attention on casting. He had seen how Ross dragged the flies slowly across the surface of the water in imitation of a swimming fly or bug. He tried this. He tried it several times. To his surprise he did not have a single strike.

Occasionally a triumphant shout came to him across the water, and he knew others in the party were having luck. He began to get impatient. He tried letting the fly sink. He tried jerking it out of the water rapidly. Nothing worked.

After a while he waded back into shore and walked along the bank, hoping for a lucky spot. At last he came to the outlet of the lake where the current was swift. To his amazement he saw trout breaking on the surface. Jeff could hardly contain his excitement. He found a place on a slippery rock and began casting. On his fifth try he succeeded in getting his fly over the spot where the fish were breaking, and before he knew he had hooked a trout.

A trout? Goodness, no. It was a whale!

He had never imagined there could be that much pull. Jeff's rod bent double. He could see the fish quite clearly, all crimson and silver. His ears were filled with the whining sound of his line reeling out, out.

It suddenly occurred to Jeff that he might lose his catch. This was such a frightening thought that he gave all his attention to playing the fish as he had just seen Ross do. The trout plunged heavily. He bored in and out. He made short runs. At one particularly sharp lunge Jeff lost his balance on the slippery rock, sat down hard, and slipped into the cold water above his knees. In his excitement he hardly noticed. The bright beautiful colors of the fish blazed as he jumped above the water. Jeff knew that he had to have him. Slowly he backed up to the bank, playing the fish along with him. The fight was going out of the creature. He was reeling him in. At last Jeff succeeded in landing him on the pebbly beach. He looked tremendous. He was beautiful, deep red and silver and green, and spotted all over.

Jeff strung a line through the gills and carried the fish back to camp. When he arrived the others in the party were returning also. They had all caught a great many fish, but they stared in amazement at Jeff's lone catch.

"Look at the size of it, will you?"

"It must weigh five and a half pounds. Jeff, you're a champion!"

"You'll have to get that stuffed and show it to your grandchildren."

Jeff laughed and then he shivered a little. He realized suddenly that he was soaked from the waist down and that a cut on his shin was bleeding.

He felt like a veteran camper when he went to the tent and put a Band-Aid on his cut and changed into dry clothes.

CHAPTER FIVE

That evening for supper they had fish. Ross and Nick knew how to prepare it expertly, and Jeff for the first time in his life decided that fish could really be delicious. They did not eat Jeff's beautiful catch. That had been put between green leaves and stored where it would be kept cool. Jeff was seriously considering the suggestion to have his trout stuffed. He could see it mounted on a board and hanging on the wall above his bed. He could take his visiting friends to his room and point proudly to the brightly colored fish and say, "See, see what I caught at Silver Lake?" The more he thought of it, the better he liked the idea.

They had eaten while it was still light for two reasons. One, they were all so desperately hungry that they could not wait. And, two, because it was a lot easier to cook and clean up while they could see.

After Ross had washed the last of the pots and utensils in the lake, he suggested to Jeff that they walk around the shore and have a look at the beaver dams. They slipped into extra jackets and Ross took along a flashlight.

"You'll have to be very quiet," warned Ross, "otherwise the beavers will dive under into their tunnels and we won't see them at all."

"You betcha," answered Jeff, the way Hugh did when he agreed to anything.

They walked for quite a while without speaking. Suddenly Ross caught hold of Jeff's sleeve and with his other hand pointed out across the smooth water. Jeff first saw a ripple in the form of a widening V. Then he saw the beaver, carrying some aspen twigs in its mouth, and swimming toward the dam.

Ross whispered, "He keeps his front feet close to his chest and paddles with his hind ones. He steers with his tail. See how flat and broad it is?"

They sat down on a rock and watched. The beaver suddenly dove under the water and disappeared.

"Where's he going?" asked Jeff.

"To the bottom of the lake. That's where the secret entrance to his tunnel is. The tunnel leads to a hole in the floor of his house. Look, there's another one swimming."

They were silent as they watched the brown head smoothly pushing through the water. Ross watched tensely. He was as excited, Jeff thought, as he himself had been when he caught the trout. This was odd because after all it wasn't anything much to get excited about. Just a beaver swimming through the water.

"Look," Ross whispered, "it's a mother beaver with two babies coming up behind. Watch 'em now, they'll dive right after her."

Of course! There were the two little heads moving right along in their mother's wake. He had been looking straight at them and not seeing them at all. He would not have seen them except for Ross.

Then the mother went under, and one, two, the babies followed. There was nothing to show that they had been there except tiny ripples on the lead-colored water.

They sat for a while longer. Ross noted the sound of frogs and katydids. It was getting dark quite rapidly. Jeff wondered if they shouldn't go back to camp. But Ross made no move. After a while he said, "I like the night. In the daytime you see things. In the nighttime you hear and smell things. Did you ever listen to dew dripping from leaf to leaf or the voice of rabbits talking?"

Jeff shook his head.

"Things smell different at night, too. The water from the lake, for instance. It's heavier and wetter somehow."

Jeff breathed deeply. Yes, Ross was right. It was heavier. He thought he noticed the rich odor of rotted wood. He spoke of this.

"Sure," Ross answered, "from the beaver's dam. It's made up of hundreds of water-soaked logs. I wish sometime you could see a beaver cutting down a tree. He does it all with his teeth. He cuts notches in the trunks, one notch about four inches below the other. Then he pulls out the piece between the notches. He does this all around the tree until it falls over. It takes him only about three minutes to cut down a tree five inches thick."

"No kidding?"

"Yeah. And that isn't all. After they cut down the tree they cut the branches off and chop the trunk up into logs. Later they carry the branches and logs to the lake. When they get them in the water they're able to tow them pretty easily to where they want them. They're wonderful animals. Always working."

"That's why people say 'busy as a beaver,' I suppose."

Ross stretched and rose. "Yep," he said. "Want to go back to camp?"

Jeff followed in Ross's footsteps. Darkness had fallen. "Do you suppose," Jeff asked after a while, "that beavers think?"

Ross stopped so abruptly that Jeff all but bumped into him. "Think!" he exclaimed indignantly, "of course they think. What ever made you imagine they didn't?"

Jeff was flustered. "I—I don't know. I just thought that maybe animals were different from humans—I don't know—people say—"

"People say," repeated Ross angrily. "Most people never stop to study animals at all. If they did, they wouldn't go around saying silly things like animals don't think or feel or have a language of their own." He switched on his flashlight and strode off the pebbly shore into a thicket of aspen.

Jeff followed silently until once more Ross stopped abruptly and ran his light up the trunk of a thick aspen. "I thought so," he said.

"What?"

"Bear marks. Pretty fresh ones too." His light played on some deep gashes in the bark about six feet from the ground.

Bear marks! Jeff had seen them during the ride up the mountain, but it had been day then. Now it was night. The bear marks looked quite different. Deep. Fierce. Cruel.

"You mean there are bears around us now?" Jeff asked, trying not to sound frightened.

"Oh, they've probably gone off a way," answered Ross carelessly. "They don't particularly like the smell of people."

"But they MIGHT be around?" he questioned again.

"They might," Ross allowed. "But look,

there's nothing to be afraid of. If you leave them alone, they'll leave you alone."

The sound of twigs snapping under their feet as they walked sounded very loud. The darkness surrounding Ross's beam of light was inky. It was all very well, Jeff thought, for Ross to say not to be afraid. Maybe Ross wasn't. But he, Jeff, was getting fear prickles all up and down his back, and he couldn't for the life of him keep from casting little darting looks into the darkness behind him.

"Of course you're not used to night," Ross continued evenly, "except inside a house with all the lights blazing. That's the way most people like it. But animals are different. The majority of them wait until night to go out."

Jeff did not find this comforting news.

"There's nothing to worry about, really," said Ross. "Animals are far less dangerous to man than cars on a busy highway."

Jeff thought this over. He decided he preferred taking his chances with the cars. He knew about cars and he didn't know about the animals.

"People are always afraid of what they don't know or understand," said Ross as if he knew Jeff's thoughts. "Once you start studying a thing you stop being frightened."

Ross was probably right. But still Jeff could not help the way he felt. The great blackness of the aspen forest was spooky. The way Ross's flashlight outlined plants and bushes leaving all the rest in unknown shadows was spookier still. He wished they'd get back to camp and the bright campfire in a hurry.

But Ross was enjoying the night walk. He pointed out a star palely glimmering through a break in the trees and stopped to listen to the soft hooting of an owl. He walked slowly, trying to make as little noise as possible. Jeff had no choice but to imitate him.

Suddenly Ross stopped dead in his tracks, and Jeff, following the line of the flashlight beam directly ahead, saw two gleaming lights shining back at them. Eyes! And then Ross's beam shifted slightly lower and picked up two more pairs!

For several moments nothing moved. Jeff could hear only the hammering of his own heart. The eyes glared out of the darkness at them.

"Bears," whispered Ross at last. "Just stand perfectly still."

Jeff did not know how long it was that they stood and stared at the eyes. It seemed forever. It seemed to him that his whole life up to this moment was something strange and far away.

"It's a mother and two cubs," whispered Ross, as if he were confiding a wonderful secret.

Jeff swallowed hard. Hadn't he heard somewhere that the mother bear was the most ferocious? What on earth might she do to them should she get the idea they intended hurting her cubs?

Ross held the flashlight steady, and still none of them moved. How much longer, Jeff wondered, would this go on? His eyes had grown accustomed to the darkness now and he could see the outline of the mother bear. She was standing up on her hind legs beside a tree and she looked enormous.

Suddenly, at some unknown signal, the cubs began to move. The sound of snapping twigs and underbrush crackled in the stillness like pistol shots. For an instant Jeff was sure that he and Ross were being attacked. He looked desperately around him, wondering in which direction he should run. But all the time, like a clock ticking firmly inside him, came the thought: Wait for Ross to give directions. And Ross stood still as before. So Jeff stood beside him.

The glaring eyes of the cubs were gone. And then all at once the mother bear's eyes disappeared and they could hear her ambling through the forest after her babies.

Jeff leaned against a tree and breathed deeply. All at once he felt very tired.

"O.K.," said Ross matter-of-factly, "let's get going."

Once more Jeff walked silently behind the older boy.

I have to hand it to you," Ross said after a while, "you sure didn't panic. Most dudes do."

"Oh," Jeff blurted out because he couldn't help himself, "I was scared to death."

"But you didn't show it," Ross said. "That's the only thing that counts, not showing it."

A warm feeling flowed through Jeff. "Gee," he said, "thanks."

Ross pushed his glasses up his nose and said with the greatest unconcern, "There's nothing to thank me for."

After that they walked without talking. When they reached camp and the big warm campfire Jeff was truly sorry to have their prowl over.

Later, when he crawled into his sleeping bag next to Ross and Nick, he listened to the sound of the owl hooting and the soft wind in the pines. They were nice sounds. He winked at a friendly star blinking at him above the aspen and fell fast asleep.

CHAPTER SIX

One evening just at dessert time Ross stormed into the dining hall. "Look," he shouted dramatically, and held a poster high so that they all could see.

Red letters in a flaming arch proclaimed "Dude Rodeo."

"Imagine!" Ross continued. "The nerve! The impudence!" He slapped his fingers across the drawing under the bold letters.

"What is it?"

The dudes crowded around Ross for a better view. Jeff got close enough to see what it was that caused Ross to be so angry.

At first look it was just a comic drawing of a horse race. There was one horse streaking ahead of all the others. There were four or five in a bunch following. And one poor, tired, unhappy animal and rider limping in at the tail end. But, horror of horrors, that poor, tired, unhappy animal carried on his hindquarter the unmistakable brand of Triangle X Ranch!

"This," said Ross with a sinister expression, "is the work of Bar Q."

"What's Bar Q?" asked Jeff.

"One of the other dude ranches competing in the rodeo. They made this poster, you can be sure. Triangle X Ranch last. Huh!" And Ross went out of the dining hall fuming.

"Well," said Mrs. Platter, "the fun's begun!"

And indeed it had.

In the days that followed Nick and Ross started training the dudes for the rodeo. As far as the Platter boys were concerned, the rodeo was no joke. They held the honor of the Triangle X very dearly and they succeeded in making their guests feel that way too. Only the best and the most willing would represent their beloved ranch.

"Do you suppose I have a chance to be in it?" Jeff questioned Hugh, as he and Luke lay sprawled on the grass back of the ranch house, resting after lunch.

"Could be."

"You ever been in a rodeo?"

"Yeah, in the days when I didn't have no sense."

"What days were those?" asked Luke, his black Indian eyes lighting with laughter.

"When I was young like you," Hugh shot back at him.

"No, really, tell me about it," begged Jeff.

"They was just no-count rodeos, I guess. Just a place to get your neck broken. You paid ten dollars down for the privilege of maybe lying in the dust or maybe winning a hundred-dollar prize."

"Did you ever win a hundred-dollar prize?"

Hugh pushed his hat to the back of his head. "Once."

"Tell me."

"Well—it was a bulldogging event."

"What's bulldogging?"

"Don't they teach you nothing in school back East?" Luke questioned.

"South, you mean," returned Jeff.

"East–South–it's all one just so long as it isn't West."

Jeff laughed. He wasn't at all sure but that Luke was absolutely right.

"Bulldogging," said Hugh, "is steer wrestling. See," he said, drawing in the dust with a stick, "the cowboy waits on his horse here. The steer is held in the chute at the end of the arena. At the signal the gate flies open and out breaks that old steer like a million wasps were after him. Well, the dogger takes after him at top speed. When he reaches the steer's flanks the cowboy quits the saddle headfirst, grabs the steer's horns, digs in his heels, and sits down, and the tussle is on. Your job's done when you've got the steer's horns on the ground and his nose pointing upward."

"And who gets the prize?"

"One who does it fastest." Hugh smiled to himself. "Seven and a half seconds flat. That's what I done it in when I won the prize money."

"Seven and a half seconds, boy!"

"Yep. Just in the time it takes you to count

to seven and a half slow-like," Hugh drawled.

Jeff counted it out to himself. He looked at Hugh with a new kind of wonder. "Don't you ever do it anymore?" he asked hopefully.

"Nope. Like I said, rodeo's a place for people who got no sense."

"Like dudes, you mean?" asked Jeff, laughing.

"Dudes!" Luke spat out the word. "That piddling stuff they do up at that Dude Rodeo. Doesn't amount to a row of coyotes."

"That's not exactly so," said Hugh, who always stuck up for the dudes against Luke. "They do pretty well up there. Of course they don't have the real dangerous stuff, but they do all right."

"I wish I could be in it," said Jeff and looked over to the corral where Bee peacefully nursed her little sorrel colt. It occurred to Jeff that Bee and her baby had been wrangled to the corral with the rest of the *remuda* every day for the past week. Did this mean that the Platter boys planned using her in the rodeo? And if so was he to race her?

Jeff did wish that someone would say something to him one way or the other. But Nick and Ross seemed too busy training the older boys and girls for the saddling race and the pack race and the novelty race or even the slow horse race. That one was really going to be a funny one. Imagine winning a race because you were slowest! But Triangle X Ranch boasted a horse that was the slowest walker in the whole valley, and nobody from another ranch had beaten him from one year to the next. Jeff had watched one of the girls practicing the slow walk. But he didn't envy her. What he wanted was speed. He looked again at Bee. She seemed so peaceful and happy with her colt. No thoughts of a race seemed to disturb her. It was odd, Jeff thought, that this gentle mother horse should be the fastest runner on the ranch.

Hugh rose from the grass and stretched himself. "Back to work." He yawned lazily. "You riding out with me this afternoon, Jeff? I was thinking of going down by Dead Man's Creek."

Jeff sprang up. "You betcha," he said. He wasn't going to miss riding to any place with such a fascinating name as Dead Man's Creek. He walked with the wranglers through the gate of the corral. Skunk nickered at him in greeting. He stroked the soft nose. "You know me now, boy, don't you? You know me now?"

Skunk nodded his head as if in answer.

Jeff buried his face against Skunk's warm neck. He was wonderfully happy. For the moment he had completely forgotten about the Dude Rodeo.

The next day Jeff was tapped.

Those Platter boys! They just never made a fuss about anything. You'd think it was something that happened every day of the world. Ross asking at breakfast, all unconcerned, between mouthfuls of pancake and sausage, "You want to ride the Kids' Pony Race, Jeff?"

Jeff almost choked on his milk. Did he want to ride the Kids' Pony Race! He tried awfully hard to be calm the way Ross was. "Sure," he said. And then he added, because he couldn't help it, "You betcha!"

"O.K. Tell Hugh to fit you out on Tiny and report up to the race track at three."

Ross had said Tiny. So it wouldn't be Bee after all. Tiny was a good fast horse too, but not so good as Bee, from all that he had heard. But if Bee could not be separated from her colt, well then he'd have to do his best on Tiny. The main thing was that he was to race. Nick and Ross had picked him as the most likely kid under twelve on the ranch. This was an honor he must do everything in his power to live up to.

Promptly at three Jeff and Tiny were at the race track. So were Ross and Nick and a couple of other kids they'd rounded up to give Jeff some competition.

The race track was a long flat stretch of land at the top of the slope back of the ranch. Each spring the track was plowed. The hoofs of many galloping horses kept the sod firm and packed. It was a fine safe place to let your horse really go. The dudes all loved the race track. But today it was reserved for training.

First of all Jeff had to get used to Tiny. She was a delicate-looking, nervous little horse, and the least pressure with his knees or kick with his heels was enough to make her spurt forward. The minute she arrived at the race track she was ready to take off. But the Platter boys would have none of that.

The start of the race was the important thing. And in this they set about training Jeff at once. They drew a starting line across the brown dirt and said briefly, "Stay back of this line until you hear the signal."

The signal was a small whistle Ross held be-

tween his teeth. He took forever before he finally blew it, because they were always getting ahead of themselves and crossing the line too soon. Or they got tangled up with each other, which made the horses nervous and fussy.

"Look," explained Nick, "if you can't hold your horse, turn him in a circle and come back again toward the starting line. You've got to keep your position. You'll get disqualified if you foul things up."

But at last the start wasn't too bad and he let them go. If Jeff had thought he'd traveled fast on Skunk across the flats, he now realized it was nothing compared to the way he was going on Tiny. For a few seconds there was dust in his eyes kicked up by the horse in front of him, but then Tiny had leaped ahead and kept it up until they seemed to be going the stretch alone. He came in way ahead of the others, but he didn't think about that one way or the other. He had somehow forgotten that it was a race. He had been too taken up with the feeling of galloping so fast. It was a wonderful, exciting feeling. He thirsted for more of it.

Ross and Nick seemed to understand. "Got to get the feel of it," was the way they put it.

Then after the horses and riders had rested a bit they let them try it again.

For several days they trained this way. Jeff always came in way ahead of the others. There was really nothing to it. He began to feel rather proud and confident.

Then Nick spoke to him. "Jeff," he said, "you're going to sleep up there on Tiny."

Sleep? He blinked unbelievingly at Nick.

"Don't get any ideas because you're coming in first so easily here in training. First of all the other kids are mounted on horses not nearly so fast as Tiny, and secondly they don't ride as well as you do. So it would be a pretty sorry thing if you weren't coming in first every time, wouldn't it?"

Jeff nodded.

"But the race at the rodeo is something else again. Each kid there will be mounted on the fastest horse from his ranch. Each kid there will be their best rider. So you see you can't afford to go to sleep."

This put rather a new light on things. Jeff felt a small nervous flutter in his stomach.

Nick smiled a little. Then he went on to

explain. "You'll have to urge your horse on more. Remember, bring the whip down on his flank at every stride. I don't mean to beat him hard, but he's got to know that you're there urging and urging him to do his best. Get it?"

He got it. It meant trying harder. Putting his mind on what he was doing every minute. Jeff thought about this a lot after they were finished training for the day. He even spoke to Hugh about it once they'd unsaddled all the horses following the dudes' afternoon ride.

Hugh gave Jeff one of his steady judging looks. "When a man works around horses," he said, "he learns to keep alert. His body and his mind seem to work like one. If he stopped to study out a thing before his body moved, he'd be a goner before he ever got started. Maybe we get to be a little like the critters ourselves. Sort of tuned to the unexpected. Ready to take a knock when it comes but keep going just the same. We don't have much time for feeling sorry for ourselves. Things like wind and snow and heavy rains and flooding gullies and hot baking sun—they don't ask no questions. They don't care about a man that whines. They don't—" Hugh broke off suddenly and laughed as he slapped Jeff on the shoulders. "Listen to me talking up a breeze, will ya?"

Jeff aimed a friendly punch to Hugh's ribs.

"That's a boy," Hugh said, as he laughingly fended Jeff off. "You just keep in there fighting."

As Jeff walked down the road to his cabin for a hot shower and a change of clothes before dinner, he thought of what Hugh had said. He thought of Nick's warnings about the coming race. And then suddenly he looked up and saw the great overpowering mountains. They were always there, but sometimes one forgot to look at them. That is, really look at them as he did now.

He approached his cabin. His mother and father sat on the steps of the porch. His father said, "He gets to look more like a wrangler every day we're here."

He did not tell them that he had heard. He just smiled at them as he passed them on the steps on the way to his room.

CHAPTER SEVEN

The morning of the Dude Rodeo was very gray. Great woolly clouds blanketed the mountains.

"Bet it's snowing up there," Jeff's father had said on their way up the path to the ranch house for breakfast.

"You don't suppose it's going to rain?" asked Jeff. "Tiny doesn't like a wet track. It makes her nervous."

"Now stop worrying," said Jeff's mother. "You know it isn't going to do a bit of good."

Mother always said that, and somehow Jeff always felt better because she did. But this morning the familiar words failed to carry their usual comfort. After all, Mother didn't know a thing about wet tracks or dry tracks or how a horse acted at a race. This was wrangler's talk. He wished that Hugh or the Platter boys were around to be consulted.

But they were all gone with the horses to Camp Robbins. They had left the afternoon before to make the twelve-mile trip, taking with them not only the horses for the races but a horse for each dude at Triangle X to ride in the grand march that started the rodeo off. It was a matter of great pride to the Platters to have all their dudes ride in the march. Everyone had purchased a red shirt and a yellow kerchief for the rodeo. These were the colors of Triangle X Ranch.

Mrs. Platter breezed into the dining room and called out a cheery "good morning" to her guests. Her hand rested lightly on Jeff's shoulder as she passed him.

"Is it going to rain?" he asked her.

"Nooo—" Her voice rang out cheerily. "Now you know it can't rain on rodeo day."

Jeff felt a little better. Still he couldn't help

thinking that Hugh would not have answered him so. Hugh would have raised his eyes slowly to the mountains and regarded them carefully for several seconds. He would have remarked on the clouds and the wind and the sun. And then finally he would have given his prediction. Good or bad, it would have been something you could put your trust in.

Later as they drove to Camp Robbins the clouds looked blacker and blacker. Jeff knew, from stories he had heard, that storms could be sudden and fierce in the valley. All the weeks he had been at the ranch the weather had been clear. But now, looking at these dark angry clouds hugging the mountains, he understood something of the awe they inspired.

"Please," he kept whispering to himself, "don't let it rain. Tiny doesn't like a wet track. Please don't let it rain."

His mother turned around in the front seat of the car and reached back to pat his hand.

Camp Robbins was a couple of miles off the highway on back dirt roads. There were signs all along the way pointing to the Dude Rodeo. At the entrance to the camp grounds Nick Platter was helping with the sale of tickets.

"We've got a big crowd in spite of the weather," he remarked.

"Is it going to rain?" Jeff questioned again, leaning out of the car window and grabbing Nick's arm in his anxiety.

"It might hold off another hour. Can't say exactly. But we'll be getting it sooner or later, I'm afraid."

"But Tiny gets nervous on a wet track," Jeff reminded Nick.

"Yeah, I know. But cheer up, Bee's here. We brought her and her colt for the milk race." And with that Nick moved to the car behind them.

Bee here. Now what did that mean? Would they give him Bee to race if the track got wet? A horse he'd never even ridden before? Bee, the fastest horse at Triangle X!

Jeff bounced up and down on the car seat. He didn't know what to think. He didn't know what to hope. He looked at the clouds now with a jumble of feelings.

The camp grounds were swarming with people and horses. Ringing the half-mile race track were trucks and horse trailers. Already spectators were taking their places on the crude benches placed on a slope boarding the track. Horses whinnied from one to another, eager for a familiar sound among all these unfamiliar *remudas.* In the center of the track a number of men on a large truck were testing the loud-speaker system. Loud bursts of band music echoed around the brown buttes. Then, abruptly, a man's voice blared, "One, two, three. Testing, one, two, three."

Jeff found Hugh at the corral marked off for Triangle X. There were eight ranches besides the camp itself competing, and there was a corral assigned to each one. Why, there must be hundreds and hundreds of horses here, Jeff thought. The air was heavy with the smell of them.

"Is Tiny all right?" Jeff asked.

"You bet," Hugh answered distractedly. He looked tired. He moved quickly from one horse to another, checking cinches.

Jeff wanted to consult Hugh about the possibility of rain and what Nick had said about Bee, but he realized suddenly that Hugh didn't have the time. Hugh had his job to do and he was doing it. All day yesterday he had worked with Val and Luke; bringing the horses the twelve-mile trek from Triangle X to Camp Robbins; getting them safely corraled; feeding and watering them; sleeping near them; again in the morning feeding and watering them; and now saddling them for the dudes to ride in the grand march. Jeff mustn't worry Hugh with his own small concerns.

Jeff led Skunk out of the corral and climbed on.

Hugh said, "Go tell our people they can mount now for the march."

Jeff was glad to trot off on his errand. It gave him something to do that would keep his mind off the coming race for a little while.

The loud-speaker system was working well now. "Everyone ready for the grand march," it announced in such wonderfully loud tones that it could be heard to the farthest corral.

All the dudes looked very gay. Triangle X all in red shirts. Bar Q in royal blue. The other ranches in black and silver, yellow, purple, orange, green, gold. If only the sun had been shining, how dazzling they would have looked!

But the sun was still in hiding. The heavy clouds, darker still, hung wrapped around the mountains. The wind had lessened almost to a whisper, as if waiting another time to show its power.

"Maybe the rain will hold off," Ross said as

he came up to Jeff. "Here, hop down and let me pin on your racing number."

"What is it?"

"Number 92. A good lucky number." Ross fastened it to the back of Jeff's red shirt. "Listen now," he went on. "Kids' Pony Race is second on the program. Soon as the grand march is over you ride back to the corral and leave Skunk. Then you get back to the starting line. We'll have your mount ready there for the race. Nick and I will be there, don't worry."

And Ross was gone before Jeff could ask a single question.

The horses all stepped lively to the band music. Mr. and Mrs. Platter carried banners at the front of the procession. The spectators clapped the ranches in. The center of the ring was reserved for the announcers and the judges and the starters. Also for the newspaper cameramen and for someone who had set up a movie camera on a tripod. It was all very exciting, and Jeff felt his stomach more fluttery than ever. Skunk too seemed to feel the excitement. He stepped at a lively pace almost as if he were trying to keep time to the music.

After the grand march they all took their horses

back to the corral. The dudes not competing in the events went to take their places on the spectator benches and cheer their friends along. Jeff hurried to the starting line as Ross had instructed him to.

Then all of a sudden it hit. A moment before there had been no wind. In the next second it whipped and blew around them, swirling the brown dust of the corrals, pelting them with raindrops so large that they made an exploding sound as they landed. Everyone ran for shelter to the nearest car.

And then just as suddenly as it had come the rain was gone. A few feeble streaks of sun shone through the gray sky.

But the track! What had happened to the track? Jeff climbed quickly out of the steamy car and ran to the track fence. Everywhere people were peeling raincoats like butterflies coming out of cocoons. The loud-speaker blared, "All right, folks, let's get started with the milk race. Get your mares and foals ready for the milk race."

Jeff stared anxiously at the track. The turf had darkened to deep brown. Here and there were a few puddles. But it was not as wet as he had dreaded. Would Tiny make it all right?

Or would those delicate little feet grow nervous and jumpy in a slithery puddle and so lose the race for Jeff and Triangle X?

Jeff saw Nick leading Bee, followed by Ross with the little colt. They crossed the track to the center ring. He called to them, but they did not hear above the music and the talking of the crowd.

Soon nine mares were at one end of the field and nine bewildered little colts were at the other end. The announcer gave the warning; a gun was fired; and the mares and colts were loosed to find one another.

What a strange and touching sight it was! Some of the mares nickered gently to their babies. A few placidly nibbled at the dry grass. Bee looked around at the crowd as if to ask what it was all about. Then she walked slowly in the direction of the colts.

The babies in the meantime reacted in their own way. A few of the youngest bleated piteously, wobbling about on their unsteady long legs. One little dark fellow took the occasion to butt his neighbor. But Bee's colt took it all in fun. He began to run around in a small circle and kick his legs in the air. He did not seem to care in the least that Bee was walking steadily toward him across the field.

In the end it was one of the youngest colts that mothered up first. Bee had to search out her young one and sniff him all over before he settled down and began to nurse. It was in this way that Bee's lighthearted colt cost Triangle X a ribbon.

Kids' Pony Race next!

Jeff walked around the track to the starting point. This was a half-mile track, but the kids' race was to be only a quarter-mile. This meant that they started at the far end of the track and ended the race just in front of the spectators' benches.

As he walked he watched anxiously as one of the judges cantered his horse around the turf. No question about it, there were spots where the mud slushed around the horses' hoofs. Tiny would hate this. What, oh what, were Ross and Nick planning to do?

At the starting line horses and riders were assembling. The royal blue of a Bar Q shirt stood out brilliantly. For a second the comic poster, showing a Bar Q racer way out front and a poor unhappy Triangle X dude bringing up the rear, flashed across Jeff's mind. It wasn't going to turn out that way really, was it? He licked his lips nervously.

Nick broke away from the group of horses and riders and walked toward Jeff. "Look," he said, putting his arm around Jeff's shoulders, "you've got something to decide. Whatever you say is O. K. Ross and I have been watching the track. It's pretty slippery for Tiny, still I think she'll make a good showing in spite of it. On the other hand, we have Bee saddled and ready. A wet track doesn't mean a thing to Bee. Strictly speaking we didn't want to race her so soon after having a colt, but you're light and won't be too much of a strain for her. Only thing is you've never ridden her. Maybe you'd rather take your chance with the horse you know. It's up to you. What do you say?"

Jeff frowned. He had counted on Ross and Nick to make the decision for him. For a second he resented that they had forced this added responsibility on him. Wasn't it enough to ride the race? He shifted uneasily from one leg to the other, gazing down at his mud-covered boots. Then, suddenly looking up, his eyes traveled over the assembled horses. The Bar Q boy was mounting a solid-looking gray. Wranglers were checking equipment. Luke, very serious and not at all his usual mocking self, was going over Tiny's bridle. Ross, near by, was tightening Bee's cinch. Everyone was completely intent on his own business. They worked swiftly, surely, and with absolute concentration.

No one was asking anyone else to do his job for him. That was the way it was out here. You stood on your own two feet—were a "regular hand," as Hugh always put it—or else!

Jeff smiled suddenly. "Make it Bee," he said, trying to have it sound very easy.

"Good enough," said Nick, and went over to the starter to inform him of the change in horses.

Jeff moved to Bee's side and stroked her neck soothingly. He could feel the excitement in the tense muscles.

Nick came back and gave Jeff a boost into the saddle. "You've got a break," he said. "You've drawn position number one next to the rail. Just see that you keep that position for the entire race. Keep your eye on the big gray Bar Q horse. He's your worst rival. Good luck."

Ross led Bee out to the starting line. He looked up at Jeff through his heavy black-rimmed glasses. "Bee won't let you down, you'll see. Give

her her head and keep her feeling your whip. Don't watch the others, just look out for yourself."

And with this warning Ross let go of Bee's bridle and disappeared off the track.

The riders were alone now. On their own entirely. The starter was warning them to get into position. This was easier said than done with nine nervous horses in the line-up. One of them was always passing over the starting line and having to be turned around and brought back. The starter issued another warning.

Bee was a larger horse than Tiny. She felt broad and somehow comforting under Jeff's legs. Still he missed the nervous fussing of Tiny's ways and wondered if maybe Bee had grown sluggish since her colt was born. Had he made the wrong decision?

But there was no time to wonder. Every second counted as they juggled around at the starting line. He must not let Bee go over the starting line before the signal or he might be disqualified. He held her in tightly. She was back a safe distance. And then all at once they all pushed forward, and the starter's voice rang out, "Ready," and then the gun exploded in Jeff's ear and they were off.

For a few seconds they were just a mass of tangled horses pushing desperately forward. Jeff's leg rubbed the length of the black horse on his right as Bee moved ahead. But in front of him the gray horse from Bar Q was cutting in from his position far to the outside. He was making his way to the rail. If he made it, he'd be right in front of Bee. Already he had forced four horses to check speed as he cut in front. He had only Bee now to beat for lead position. The seriousness of the situation came in a clear flash to Jeff.

Up to this second Bee had done the thinking. But it was now Jeff's turn to take over. He must see to it they kept their rail position in the lead. This was all-important and his responsibility as the rider. He raised himself slightly higher in his stirrups and brought his whip down on Bee's flanks in the steady rhythm Ross had taught him.

The good horse pressed her speed. She hugged the rail. Not for an instant did she flinch as the big gray bore down upon her, trying to squeeze his way into the favored position. Forward. Forward. For a second Jeff thought he and the gray would collide. But with another amazing burst of speed Bee went on. And then they were alone on the track. Or so it seemed. Nothing lay ahead but the long stretch of turf and the stands at the finish line. A wonderful feeling of freedom and speed came to Jeff, and he realized fleetingly that he was enjoying himself.

From far off he heard his own name. "Jeff Mayberry from Triangle X Ranch in the lead." Of course, the loud-speaker! As he galloped he heard, "Bar Q in second position. Watch this big gray round the bend."

Jeff applied the whip harder. No big gray from Bar Q was going to overtake him at the bend.

He heard the screaming then. It was like a big ocean wave breaking over him. They were screaming for him. For him and Bee and Triangle X Ranch!

On the home stretch he looked back. He could not resist it. Just a quick turn of the head. And then he saw he had it made. The race was his and Bee's. The screaming rose to a huge roar. Over it all the loud-speaker, "The winner—Jeff Mayberry from Triangle X Ranch!"

Over the finish line he tried to draw Bee in. She was too excited to stop at once. They were a quarter of the way around the track again before he had her pulled in.

"Come get your ribbons at the finish line."

Jeff cantered back. He grasped his blue ribbon proudly. He saw his father almost under Bee's nose shooting pictures with his movie camera. Everyone shouted congratulations. All his friends from Triangle X were jumping up and down with excitement. It was a grand moment.

Outside the track Hugh came and held Bee's bridle as he dismounted.

"You did O. K., boy," he said quietly.

The look in Hugh's steady gray-blue eyes, as he smiled at him, made Jeff's joy complete.

CHAPTER EIGHT

Dusty jeans and jackets and scuffed boots were stuffed into the duffel bag. How quickly, Jeff thought, all his belongings were cleared from this cabin room he had grown so to love during his weeks at the ranch. It wasn't a room like his room at home, full of toys and pictures and mementos of sports. Not a room to be in by the hour. Just a place to sleep and change clothes. A place to get ready for the things happening outside that were important.

And now they were leaving. The room was bare, the way it had been when he arrived. In a few hours he would be flying high above the mountains far, far away from all this. The weeks at the ranch would seem like a dream.

"Will you forget me?" he had asked Hugh the day before.

"Not likely," Hugh had answered. "And you won't be forgetting us. Cheer up, Jeff. You'll be taking part of the ranch home with you, here and here." And Hugh had lightly touched his head and his heart. "It'll be there always and no man can take it away from you."

Jeff pulled the duffel bag together. Yes, that was what Hugh had said. No man could take the remembrance of the ranch away from him. And in the next second Jeff thought of his fish—his beautiful deep red and silver and green trout—wonderfully stuffed by the taxidermist and mounted on a fine wood plank. Then he thought of his glossy blue ribbon which Mother had wrapped in tissue paper and placed for special safety in her own suitcase. And he could see quite clearly just where he was going to put both of them in his room. In that instant he wished himself home so he could be immediately about it.

"All packed?" Dad called from the porch.

"Except for my cowboy hat. May I wear it?"

"You bet," Dad answered.

And Jeff smiled to himself to hear Dad answer him in the same words one of the wranglers would have used.

Dad said to make the good-byes clean and sharp.

In the corral Hugh and Luke and Val were saddling up horses for the morning ride. Jeff suddenly felt shy wearing his traveling suit and his newly shined shoes. He stood at the corral gate and stared at his friends.

Luke saw him first. "Ah, the dude goes home." His voice was teasing.

Hugh slapped a saddle on a horse's back. "You look right sharp, Jeff." He drew the cinch up under the horse's belly. "Send us a postcard of a palm tree, now remember." Then, giving the horse a slight slap on the hindquarters, he made his way to the gate. He leaned over and took Jeff's hands between his own. "Hurry back to us next summer, Jeff. You know we always need a regular hand around here."

"A regular hand." Jeff thought of Hugh's words all the way to the airport.

Nick helped them into the airport building with their bags. He stayed with them until the big plane swooped down into the valley. Everything looked much as it had when they arrived, except that the mountains did not have as much snow on their peaks. It looked the same and yet it was all quite different. It was part of him, he thought, part of him now forever.

The passengers mounted the gangway. Jeff pulled his wide hat more firmly down on his head.

The stewardess smiled at him. "Going home, cowboy?" she asked.

Jeff nodded. And then, with one last look across the great wide range, he added to himself, "But I'll be back."